Grandpa Hunktrumpet

Gideon Rigal

meadowside
CHILDREN'S BOOKS

HUNK-a-DING! HUNK-a-DONG!

went the doorbell.

It was Grandpa Hunktrumpet's birthday and Grandma had invited Ludwig to keep him out of trouble.

Up in the attic Grandpa Hunktrumpet kept reminding himself to forget that no one had remembered his birthday.

He was rummaging through piles of dusty memories, which just happened to include some old birthday cards, when Ludwig bounced in.

"Ah, Ludwig, my boy! Come and feast your eyes over this treasure!"

"Now this is a great place to begin.
Who could forget the golden days of
'The Hunks'?" smiled Grandpa Hunktrumpet
"Who were the Hunks, Grandpa?" asked Ludwig.

"GREAT! My Hunkercycle!
I'll never forget the big top!

The thrills and spills of
us daring Trunkrobats!"

CRASH!

"Ha ha! Nice to see I haven't lost my touch!"

"Oooh, and the tales I could tell you about this, Ludwig!

Sailing the stormy seas, protecting my treasure - my prize currant buns - from those brassy bucktoothed pirates! They never did grasp the finer points of proper tea making!"

"And my Hunkbasket!

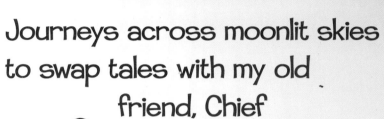

Journeys across moonlit skies to swap tales with my old friend, Chief Hunkawumpa.

I never quite got the hang of that smoke signal business though. Kept singeing my toes... and muddling my messages!"

"Oh yes, and then there was the time I tried to bungie jump with knicker elastic belonging to your Grandma! She keeps it safe in her bottom draw now, because..."

"GRANDPA HUNKTRUMPET"

"What's that?!
Sorry Ludwig, I'll have to keep
that story for another day."

"SURPRISE GRANDPA HUNKTRUMPET"

"Hoo-har, Grandma! Turn up the volume on that hunkaphone... there's some dancing to be done!"

Everyone HAD remembered...
...and everyone WOULD remember Grandpa Hunktrumpet's
HUNKTRUMPETING BIRTHDAY!

for
Jen
G.R.

First published in 2004
by Meadowside Children's Books
185 Fleet Street,
London EC4A 2HS

Text and Illustrations © Gideon Rigal 2004
The right of Gideon Rigal to be identified as the author and illustrator
of this work has been asserted by him in accordance with
the Copyright, Designs and Patents Act, 1988

A CIP catalogue record for this book is available
from the British Library.
Printed in India

10 9 8 7 6 5 4 3 2 1